Captain Noah's Zoo

ISBN 978-1-64559-627-1 (Paperback)
ISBN 978-1-64559-628-8 (Digital)

Covenant Books, Inc.
11661 Hwy 707
Murrells Inlet, SC 29576
www.covenantbooks.com

WRITTEN BY

MICHAEL PRICE

ILLUSTRATED BY

MISHA JOVANOVIC

HELLO THERE! I'M MICHAEL.

I WANTED TO PUT TOGETHER A BOOK THAT HAD AN ENTERTAINING STORY AND FUN IMAGERY. MY GOAL WAS TO HAVE A LOT OF SMILING, LAUGHING, AND CONVERSATION BETWEEN YOU AND YOUR CHILDREN AND GRANDCHILDREN WHILE EXPERIENCING THIS BOOK. THIS BOOK IS MEANT FOR AGES THREE AND UP, AND UP, AND UP... BASICALLY EVERYONE! I REALLY DO HOPE YOU ENJOY THE STORY OF ZOO ISLAND.

SO HAVE A WONDERFUL TIME!

ALL OUR FRIENDS WERE ON BOARD AND REALLY EXCITED!
THEY HAD ALL OF THE VEGGIES THEY COULD
EAT, AND CAPTAIN NOAH EVEN BROUGHT SOME
GAMES FOR THEM TO PLAY TO MAKE IT FUN.

BUT ALONG THE WAY, CAPTAIN NOAH
AND ALL THE ANIMALS HEARD
A LOUD **BANG, POOF, SMASH** FROM THE BACK OF THE BOAT.
THE SEA PICKLE'S DOOHICKEY GASKET BLEW UP!

NOW I HAVE NO IDEA WHAT THAT
IS, BUT IT TURNS OUT IT'S
REALLY, REALLY IMPORTANT!

4

NOT TO WORRY, FRIENDS! THE SEA PICKLE DRIFTED SAFELY TO A BEAUTIFUL ISLAND THAT CAPTAIN NOAH NICKNAMED

Zoo island

NOW THAT WE HAVE ALL THAT SETTLED, LET ME EXPLAIN TO YOU HOW OUR FRIENDS GET ALL THE THINGS THEY NEED. **PRESENTING...**

THINGS 'N' STUFF

ROLLER SKATES

-50%

ONCE ALL OUR FRIENDS GOT SETTLED ON THE ISLAND, THEY ORDERED ALL THE STUFF THEY NEEDED FROM A CATALOG CALLED **THINGS 'N' STUFF.**

DIY CANNON KIT

SUPER DUPER JETPACK 2000

+ **FREE**

THEIR PACKAGES WERE DELIVERED BY **THE BIRD UNION-LOCAL #1.** EVERYBODY ABSOLUTELY LOVE THESE BIRDS, BUT THERE WAS A PROBLEM, A VERY BIG PROBLEM. THESE BIRDS WERE TERRIBLE, AND I MEAN TERRIBLE, AT DELIVERING PACKAGES! LET ME EXPLAIN...

SNORKEL SET

HOPTER CHOPTER

HURRY ONLY 1 LEFT

"ARE YOU OKAY?

YOU NEED TO BE MORE CAREFUL, PIDGEY."

DO YOU SEE THAT PENGUIN SITTING ON TOP OF EDWIN? THAT'S OSCAR. HE FELL ASLEEP AND MISSED HIS BOAT, THE **SS FRIDGINATER**, SO CAPTAIN NOAH STUCK HIM ON *THE SEA PICKLE* WITH US!

16

NOW WE TRY TO HAVE FUN ON THE ISLAND. ONE OF THE THINGS WE DO IS HAVE A TALENT CONTEST ONCE IN A WHILE CALLED **THE HONK SHOW**. I'M GOING TO SHARE A STORY WITH YOU ABOUT A TIME WHERE IT DIDN'T GO SO WELL FOR ONE OF THE CONTESTANTS...AND THAT CONTESTANT WAS ERNIE.

NOW ONE OF THE THINGS THAT HAPPENS IS IF ONE OF THE CONTESTANTS IS REALLY, REALLY BAD, THEN THEY **HONK** THEM WITH THE HORNS THEY HAVE ON THEIR DESK...MEANING, YOU HAVE TO LEAVE. ERNIE WASN'T HAVING IT.

TAP TAP TAP TAP

NOW IT'S TIME TO INTRODUCE YOU TO MORE OF MY GOOD FRIENDS. LET ME TELL YOU ABOUT MUMPY. HE'S GOING THROUGH A COWBOY PHASE AND STARTED TRYING TO LASSO AND RIDE THE OSTRICHES. WELL, WILLARD HAD TO TRY TO PUT A STOP TO IT.

"I'LL MAKE A DEAL WITH YOU, MUMPY. IF YOU QUIT SNEAKING UP ON US AND TRYING TO LASSO US ALL THE TIME, I'LL LET YOU RIDE AROUND ON MY BACK ONCE IN A WHILE, OKAY?"

"CAN I PUT REINS ON YOU?"

"AND YOU'LL STOP TRYING TO LASSO US?"

"OH YEAH, AND A SADDLE?"

"**FINE**! AS LONG AS YOU DON'T TRY TO LASSO ANYBODY, I'LL LET YOU. OKAY?"

"I PROMISE! I PROMISE!"

WELL, A COUPLE DAYS LATER, WILLARD SAW MUMPY TRYING TO LASSO ONE OF THE OTHER OSTRICHES AND DIDN'T LET MUMPY RIDE HIM FOR TWO WEEKS! MUMPY DEFINITELY LEARNED HIS LESSON! MUMPY DID APOLOGIZE, BUT THAT'S WHAT HAPPENS WHEN YOU BREAK YOUR PROMISE.

DID I TELL YOU ABOUT WHEN I SAW HIM RIDING A **DOLPHIN**? WELL, THAT'S A WHOLE DIFFERENT STORY! BUT RIGHT NOW I'M GOING TO TELL YOU ABOUT OUR YOUNGEST MONKEY FRIEND, CHARLIE!

CHARLIE WALKED TO NINAL AND MUMPY WITH A VERY SAD LOOK ON HIS FACE, WITH A FOOTBALL HELMET UNDERNEATH HIS ARM.

"WHAT'S THE MATTER, CHARLIE? AND WHAT'S UP WITH THE FOOTBALL HELMET?"

"YEP, I GOT SOME BAD NEWS, FELLAS. I FELL OUT OF THE TREES TOO MANY TIMES, SO I FAILED TREE CLIMBING 101 AGAIN. IF YOU FAIL, YOU GET AN HONORABLE MENTION AND THIS BROKEN COCONUT TROPHY. THEY GAVE ME THIS FOOTBALL HELMET AND TOLD ME TO KEEP PRACTICING."

GEEZ, IT'S NEVER BORING AROUND HERE. THAT'S FOR SURE! OKAY, FRIENDS, BEFORE WE MOVE ON, I GOTTA TELL YOU ABOUT A LITTLE NATIVE CRUSTACEAN THAT'S BEEN TAGGING ALONG SINCE WE GOT HERE. THE PROBLEM IS, NOBODY EVER KNEW WHAT IN THE WORLD HE WAS SAYING.

NOW WE DO! WELL, AT LEAST A LITTLE BIT.

UMMM, THE LITTLE FELLA IS HAPPY, THAT'S FOR SURE. BUT DOES ANYBODY KNOW WHAT HE'S ACTUALLY SAYING?

YEP, THAT'S **EMOJINEZE**!

HIS NAME IS MR. PINCHY, AND HE SAYS IT'S HIS BIRTHDAY!

IT WAS ALSO SHERMAN'S BIRTHDAY, AND ALL THE ANIMALS HAD ALREADY CHIPPED IN AND GOT HIM A JET PACK AND ROLLER SKATES SO HE COULD KEEP UP WITH ALL HIS FRIENDS, CUZ HE'S A TURTLE, AND WELL, TURTLES ARE SLOW. REALLY SLOW. OH, OH, OH...LOOKY! HERE COMES CHESTER WITH SHERMAN'S GIFTS NOW!

31

OH YEAH, I ALMOST FORGOT! THAT CONTRAPTION ON ABIGAIL'S HEAD IS SOMETHING CALLED THE HOPTER CHOPTER. ABIGAIL LOVES IT. I'LL TELL YOU ALL ABOUT IT WHEN YOU COME BACK TO SEE US. FAREWELL, FRIENDS!

38